PRISCILLA LAMONT is the highly regarded illustrator
of many children's picture books, including the nursery rhyme collection
Baby Rhyme Time, and Michael Rosen's *Lovely Old Roly,* both
for Frances Lincoln. Her other book in the Nursery Rhyme Crimes series
is *Tom, Tom, the Piper's Son.* She also illustrated *Goose and Duck*
by Jill Craighead George for Harper Collins US.
She lives in Chilham, Kent.
Discover more about Priscilla's books on
www.priscillalamont.com

For Jacquie R.

JANETTA OTTER-BARRY BOOKS

LITTLE BO PEEP copyright © Frances Lincoln Limited 2011
Text and illustrations copyright © Priscilla Lamont 2011

First published in Great Britain in 2011 and in the USA in 2012 by
Frances Lincoln Children's Books, 4 Torriano Mews,
Torriano Avenue, London NW5 2RZ
www.franceslincoln.com

First paperback edition published in 2012

A catalogue record for this book is available from the British Library

ISBN 978-1-84780-354-2

Illustrated with pen and watercolour
Set in Chalkboard

Printed in Heshan, Guangdong, China by Leo Paper Products Ltd. in July 2012

1 3 5 7 9 8 6 4 2

Nursery Rhyme Crimes

Little Bo Peep

by the sheep
as told to
PRISCILLA LAMONT

F

FRANCES LINCOLN
CHILDREN'S BOOKS

Little Bo Peep has lost her sheep
and doesn't know where to find them.
Leave them alone and they'll come home,
bringing their tails behind them.

"I'm bored!" cried Little Bo Peep that day.
"Play hide-and-seek with me."
We should have known it would end in tears –
sheep don't do games, you see.

She told us to hide while she counted to ten.
She said, "It'll all be such fun."

We tried our very best to hide

but she found us before we'd begun.

Then it was our turn to count up to ten,
which none of us knew how to do.

So we followed her round wherever she went,
while she moaned, "You haven't a clue!"

We practised for hours until in the end
we'd hidden ourselves quite away.

And Little Bo Peep couldn't find us at all though she looked for us all day!

We watched as the farmer, his son and his wife were invited to join in the fun.

A policeman turned up in the end, but still
no sheep were found, not a one!

When we came out from where we were hid,
how surprised they all were, to be sure.

But it seems that Bo Peep was sent home in disgrace –
you would think that she'd broken the law!

We know she wasn't too good at her job,
but we think it's rather a shame.
We were all having such fun on the hill
while Little Bo Peep got the blame.

MORE BOOKS BY PRISCILLA LAMONT
FROM FRANCES LINCOLN CHILDREN'S BOOKS

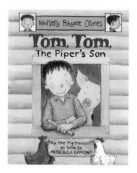

Nursery Rhyme Crimes
Tom, Tom, the Piper's Son

Tom, Tom, the Piper's son
Stole a pig and away he run. . .
But was Tom really a thief, or was he just trying to rescue
his favourite pig? Find out what happened that day
at the farm in this funny and delightful subversion
of the well-known nursery rhyme.

Baby Rhyme Time

"A lovely collection of rhyme and lullabies.
The dreamy illustrations merge perfectly
with the well-known words. . ."
Carousel

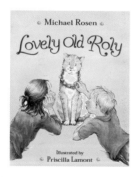

Lovely Old Roly
Story by Michael Rosen
Illustrated by Priscilla Lamont

Roly is the children's special pet, their much loved cat.
But Roly is getting old and at last it's time to say goodbye.
But after a while, it could be time to say hello to a new
kitten in the family. A beautifully told story for younger
children which helps to explain the cycle of life and loss.

Frances Lincoln titles are available from all good bookshops.
You can also buy books and find out more about your favourite titles,
authors and illustrators on our website: www.franceslincoln.com